Demoli
Dang

by Kay Woodward
Illustrated by Bill Ledger

OXFORD
UNIVERSITY PRESS

In this story ...

Jin
(Swoop)

Jin has the power to fly. He once had a race with a jumbo jet ... and won! He can fly high enough to reach outer space!

Cam
(Switch)

Axel
(Invisiboy)

The Head
(head teacher)

Chapter 1:
Three hours until demolition ...

Jin and Axel were playing super-tag.

"Now you see me ..." said Axel, running away from Jin. "Now you don't!" With a chuckle, Axel vanished.

"That's not fair!" cried Jin, crossing his arms. "How can we play tag if you're invisible?"

"OK," said Axel, reappearing on the other side of the room. "Here I am!"

Jin flew across the room to catch Axel.

He zoomed past Cam, knocking a nature book out of her hands. "Oops! Sorry," he said, picking it up. "Why don't you play super-tag? It's way more exciting than reading about newts."

"Not this one," Cam said, pointing at a picture of a newt with a red tummy and a blue crest. "The blue-crested newt is really rare. It's a protected species and ..."

Suddenly, an announcement boomed over the speakers. "All pupils must come to the school hall at once!"

Jin hurried after the others. "This sounds *bad*," he thought.

As soon as the heroes had sat down in the school hall, the Head's face appeared from a holo-projector on a table. He looked serious. "Ray Ranter is causing trouble again," he said.

"Uh oh," murmured Jin.

Everyone knew about Ray Ranter. He was horribly rich and horribly mean. Even worse, he didn't like Hero Academy one bit.

Ray Ranter

Catchphrase: Heroes are zeroes!

Hobbies: stamp collecting. He would love nothing more than to have a set of Ranter stamps.

Likes: white rooms, white suits, turnips (because they're white).

Dislikes: all colours, and raspberries (because they're hairy, and raspberry stains are impossible to remove from white suits).

Beware! He created robotic rabbits – bunny-wunnies – to help him carry out his dastardly plans.

"I'm sorry to say that Ray Ranter has come up with a fiendish plan to get rid of Hero Academy," said the Head. "Look at this."

A newspaper article was projected onto a screen on the wall.

RANTER'S NEW SHOPPING CENTRE

Ray Ranter will start demolishing Capability Way today at 11am. In its place, he will build the biggest shopping centre Lexis City has ever seen.

Capability Way was where the secret entrance to Hero Academy (Door 62) was located.

Jin gasped. "If Capability Way is destroyed, Hero Academy will be destroyed too."

"We're in a tricky situation," replied the Head. "If we speak up, everyone will find out about us – and superhero schools need to stay super-secret!"

Jin was horrified. Only Ray Ranter could come up with such a dastardly plan.

Chapter 2:
Two hours until demolition ...

"What are we going to do?" groaned Jin.

He was holding an emergency meeting with Cam and Axel outside the school in Capability Way. No one had any brilliant ideas. Things were looking grim.

"They're getting ready to start the demolition!" said Axel.

They stared in horror as a yellow crane chugged up the street. Hanging from it was a giant wrecking ball attached by a thick cable.

"Let me sort this out," said Cam. "I'll change into a rhino and knock the wrecking ball out of the way!"

Jin shook his head. "A rhino! In Lexis City? They'd call the zoo at once."

"I'll become invisible," said Axel. "Then I'll take the keys so they can't use the crane."

Jin shook his head sadly. "They'll probably have spare keys."

Axel's face fell. "Good point," he said.

Jin turned to his friends. "I wish I could help," he said sadly, "but I don't know how!" Jin decided to take to the sky. "I'm going to fly around for a bit," he said. "Flying always helps me think. Who knows, I might come up with a brilliant idea to stop the demolition."

Jin circled high above Capability Way. Below, he could see a woman walking a dog in the small park opposite Door 62 (the secret entrance to Hero Academy). The dog was barking at something near the overgrown pond. Jin swooped a little closer.

"Come here!" cried the dog's owner, dragging her pet away. "Leave it alone!"

"Hmm," murmured Jin. "What's going on?"

Jin waited until the woman and her dog were gone before landing beside the pond. He peered through the weeds. Suddenly, he spotted something. It was a newt. "Wow!" Jin said.

The creature had a red tummy and a blue crest. Jin recognised it from Cam's nature book. "You're a blue-crested newt!" he exclaimed.

The newt flicked out its purple tongue.

"You're a protected species," Jin whispered. "That means the place where you live is protected too. If Ray Ranter tried to build here, he would be breaking the law."

Jin began to smile. Perhaps there was a way to save the school after all!

Chapter 3:
One hour until demolition ...

"It *was* here," Jin muttered. He'd brought Cam and Axel straight back to see the blue-crested newt, but it was nowhere to be found.

"Well, it isn't here now," said Cam. "Never mind, Jin. It was a really good idea."

"So, let me get this right," said Axel. He looked towards the crowd of reporters and the film crew who were gathering to watch the demolition. "If one of them sees the newt, Capability Way can't be knocked down?"

Jin nodded. "That's right ... Hang on, why are you smiling?"

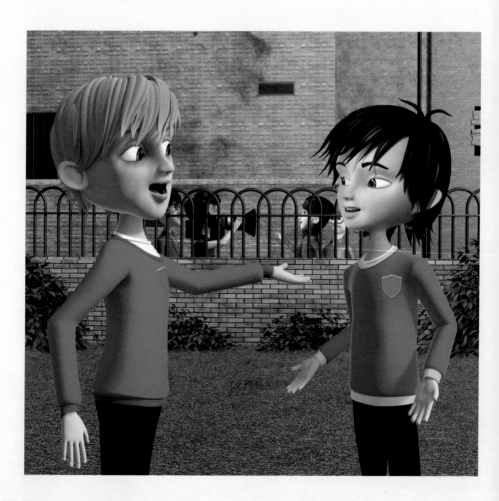

Jin followed Axel's gaze as he looked at Cam. Then Jin began to smile too. "Are you both thinking what I'm thinking?" he asked.

Cam grinned at him. "Absolutely!"

She screwed her eyes tightly shut and, as quick as a flash, she had shape-shifted. She was now a small newt with a red tummy and a blue crest.

With a nod to the boys, Cam scuttled on to a rock next to the pond.

Jin and Axel watched from behind a shady oak tree. They waited for ages, but no one spotted the tiny newt sitting on the rock.

Jin couldn't help smiling when he saw the expression on the newt's face. "I didn't think it was possible for a newt to look cross!" he said.

Axel sighed. "No one is looking at the park. They're too busy watching the wrecking ball."

Suddenly, Jin had an idea. "Watch Cam to make sure she's OK," he said to Axel, "I'll be back soon."

Jin slipped back through Door 62 and into Hero Academy. Then he went to the IT room and sat down at a computer. He tapped the keys. He clicked the mouse here and there. At last, he smiled. His leaflet was perfect!

Stop Ray Ranter from destroying the newt's habitat!

Come to Capability Way now!

☐ Say **NO** to the new shopping centre.

☐ Say **Yes** to the blue-crested newt.

Jin printed out lots of copies of the leaflet.
He looked at his watch. The wrecking ball would
begin swinging in just over half an hour. He had
to hurry!

Chapter 4:
Half an hour until demolition ...

Jin spun into his superhero costume and became Swoop. He flew into Lexis City and poked a leaflet through an open window at Lexis City School.

Swoop whizzed to Lexis City Wildlife Park and pinned a leaflet to every signpost. He stuck one to the noticeboard at Lexis City Animal Sanctuary too.

Swoop rocketed around the city, delivering leaflets to every school and to all the houses and shops near Capability Way.

Then he flew back to the park, dodged behind a tree and changed out of his superhero costume.

"Phew!" said Jin, running up to Axel.

"What have you been up to?" his friend asked.

"Just watch and see," Jin replied.

The diggers' engines were revving, ready to go. The construction workers were putting their hard hats on. The wrecking ball was slowly swinging to and fro.

Jin hopped from foot to foot. Would his plan work in time, or had it all been for nothing?

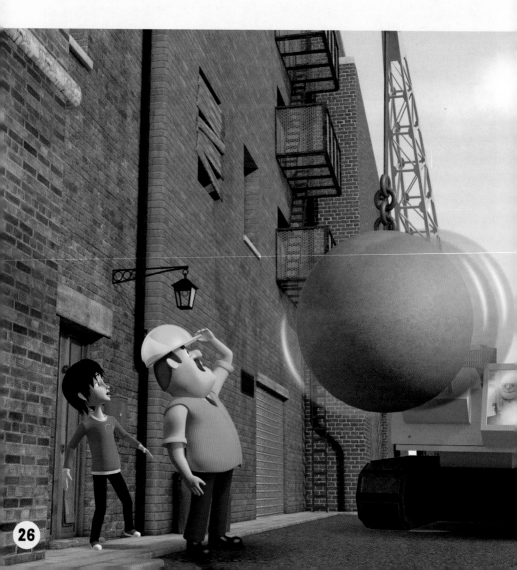

At that moment, Ray Ranter arrived in a long, white car. He got out, looked at the wrecking ball, and shouted, "GO!"

"STOP!" someone yelled.

Jin spun around. There was a huge crowd of people walking down Capability Way. "STOP!" they cried again, waving Jin's leaflets in the air.

"Stop? Why?" Ranter demanded.

"This leaflet says that blue-crested newts live here," a man from the Newt Protection Society explained. "They're a rare species. You can't destroy their home."

"Rubbish," Ranter said with a laugh. "There are no blue-crested newts here."

"Look!" shouted Jin, pointing towards the pond. "There's one!"

Everyone spun round. The photographers took pictures of the newt.

"Stop the machines now!" said the reporter.

Ranter's face turned as red as the newt's tummy. "Just stick it in a zoo and swing the wrecking ball!"

The man from the Newt Protection Society bent down to look more closely. He lifted up a leaf. "There isn't just one newt," he said. "There's a whole family of them."

"Which one is Cam?" whispered Axel.

"I have no idea!" Jin whispered back.

"I'm from the mayor's office!" cried a woman with a clipboard. "Stop the wrecking ball! You can't build a shopping centre here."

"You ... you haven't heard the last of me!" spluttered Ray Ranter.

He climbed into his car, and it zoomed away.

A few seconds later, Cam appeared beside Jin and Axel. "Great job, Jin!" she said.

Jin grinned. "I bet this will be on the front page of every *newts*paper tomorrow!"

Cam frowned. "Eh?"

"*Newts*paper … newspaper … get it?"

Cam groaned and rolled her eyes.